Make Room for Grandma Bailee:
Attack of the Walkabeeans

Written by
LaNette Shipley and Marissa Marie

Illustrations by
Michelle Adu-Asah

To order additional copies of this book, contact:
Xlibris
1-888-795-4274
www.Xlibris.com
Orders@Xlibris.com

ISBN: Softcover   978-1-7960-5583-2
        EBook   978-1-7960-5584-9

Print information available on the last page

Rev. date: 11/27/2019

Dedicated to our granddarlings,
Sammy, Shanese, Isaiah, Marissa, and heavenly baby Bryan,
and our little flower petals,
Kaylee, Addison, Paisley, and baby Zoe, for all
the many adventurous summers to come!
May God's mighty coverings bless you forever. I love you.

Love,
Your very young grandma

Grandma Bailee is a typical, sweet silver-and-charcoal-haired grandma with glasses who—along with her little fur baby, Bunzee—tries hard to keep busy helping others.

Grandma felt a bit lonely these days since her sweet husband, Hershel, went away last winter to live in heaven. Now all Grandma had left were memories of him and the twelve amazing summer adventures they had when their four grandchildren came to visit.

This sunny summer Sunday afternoon, Grandma returned home from church and decided to bake brownies for the new neighbors who had just moved in two doors down on Cadbury Lane.

While standing in the pantry, she realized the cocoa powder can was empty.

"What?" she thought. "It was a brand-new can! Where did that cocoa powder go?" She felt tired and did not want to go back to the store. With a big sigh, Grandma leaned against the pantry wall, looked at Bunzee, and wanted to cry; instead, she blurted out, "Oh, Sweetzsam, Snoogleegoo, Zaiahbooloo, Tootletoots, where could it be?"

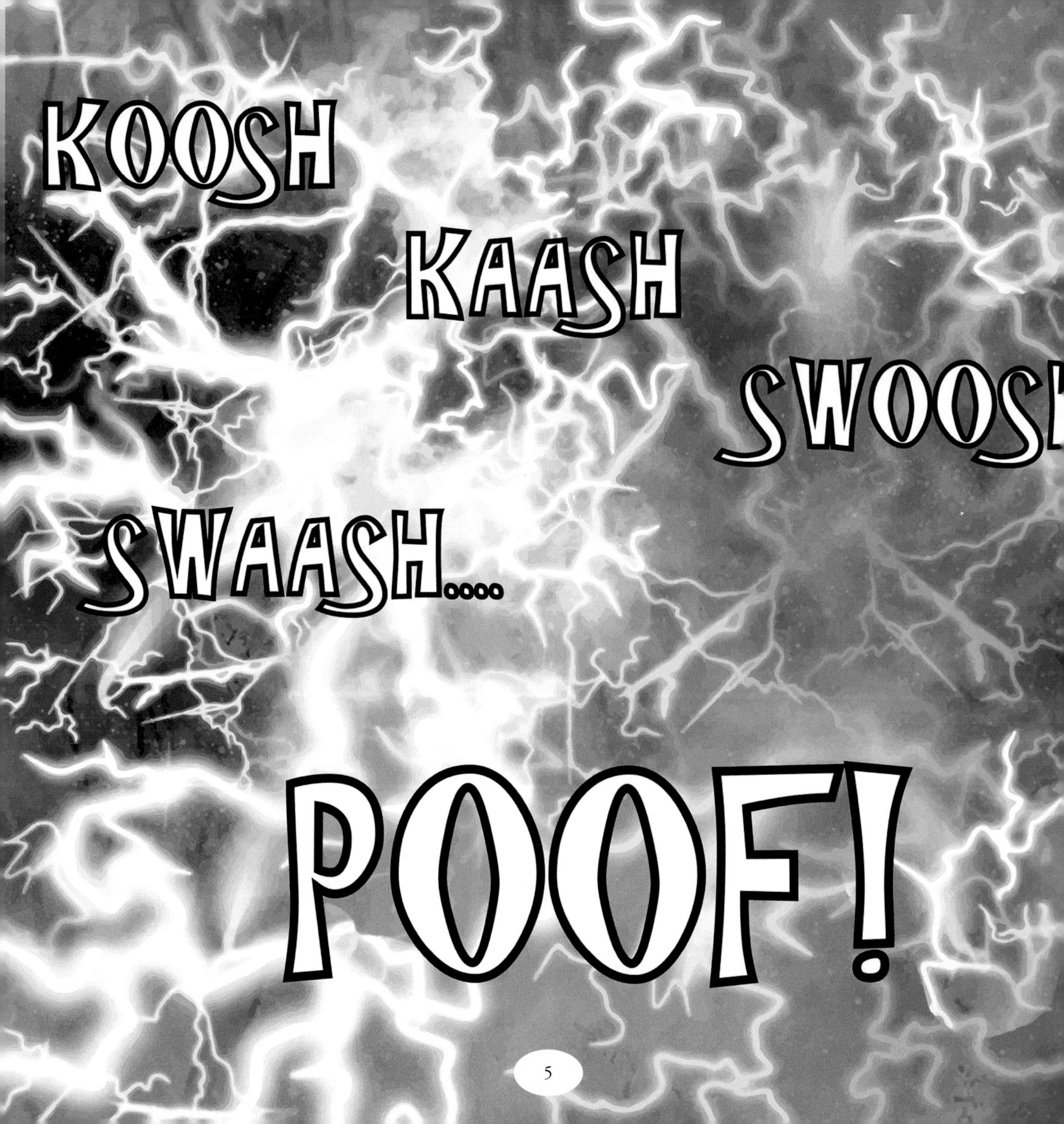
KOOSH
KAASH
SWOOS
SWAASH....
POOF!

As the last word fell from her voice, the pantry wall began to shake with a koosh, kaash, swoosh, swaash, poof!

Grandma stood in sheer amazement as the pantry wall opened up. Without fear, Grandma and Bunzee walked right through the opening into a beautiful field of evergreen trees that stood sixteen to twenty-five feet tall.

It was then Grandma Bailee realized they must have been transported to South America where these specific trees—known as cocoa trees, which grew cocoa beans—are found. These particular beans are harvested to make cocoa powder.

Wow! Could this really be happening? Grandma thought. Grandma Bailee felt very excited, as if butterflies were in her tummy, but despite being a little nervous, she was grateful to have Bunzee with her.

The trees were colorfully decorated with brown, reddish-orange, and yellow football shapes known as pods, where the cocoa beans grew safely inside, and looked like large brown seeds. Smiling with enchantment, Grandma Bailee walked among the cocoa trees, admiring the beauty of the cocoa pods.

The pods hung from the branches like fruit or Christmas tree decorations. There were many new smells for Bunzee as she sniffed along. What Grandma Bailee and Bunzee didn't realize was that they were being watched.

Do you know what a cocoa pod is?

(Most answers to questions are in the story and listed in the back.)

Without any warning, the bright blue sky opened up and down came a splatter of rain. It rains a lot in parts of South America because the cocoa trees need about four inches of rain per month in order to grow the most perfect beans. These beans are used to create cocoa powder, which Grandma Bailee needed to make the brownies.

Grandma Bailee and Bunzee were not prepared for the rain, and they tried to find cover under the cocoa leaves. But the splashing rain danced all over their bodies, causing them to shiver.

As fast as the hard rain started, it slowed to a light drizzle, then ceased as if the hand of heaven had reached down and caught the falling rain. By now, the pantry was nowhere to be seen. Grandma Bailee and Bunzee were confused and unsure of what to do or where to go next.

Grandma and Bunzee began to relax after the thundershower. But before they could catch their breath—oooooh yikes!—a frightful twist of commotion broke out, and they found themselves surrounded by the most peculiar bright, colorful blue and brown spotted creatures. The fuzzy beasts with very large yellow teeth were snarling and pointing long, sharp spears at Grandma and Bunzee. Grandma Bailee and Bunzee were very scared. Grandma, looking at the creatures, was wide-eyed in fear, and she prayed in silence.

After her prayer, with a sigh, Grandma extended the creatures a warm, bright, loving smile. Grandma soon learned that the hairy individuals could speak and were named the Walkabeeans, and they were created to protect the cocoa beans that grew inside the pods, which adorn the cocoa fruit trees. The Walkabeeans realized that neither they nor the trees were in any danger from Grandma and Bunzee.

Once the Walkabeeans realized Grandma and Bunzee were kind and of no threat to them or the trees, they dropped their spears, and they all ventured off to the village where the Walkabeeans lived in huts made of old wood and leaves from old cocoa trees. What Grandma saw overwhelmed her. There were many more Walkabeeans of different colors and sizes; some were boys, and some were girls. Some were even old and gray. It was an amazing sight!

Is cocoa part of the fruit or vegetable family?

Soon they all gathered around and prepared to share a meal together. Grandma felt concerned when she realized all that the creatures ate were food made from cocoa. Since cocoa is very bitter, it needs a lot of sugar and butter to make sweet, palatable chocolate for cooking.

"Oh my, this is not a healthy diet!" Grandma exclaimed. So she suggested the Walkabeeans go gather other fruits and vegetables from the many surrounding fields. She told them it was very important to enjoy the chocolate as a treat only on special occasions and in moderation.

The older, gray furry leader of the Walkabeeans, Lintruffleloo, spoke up. "Grandma Bailee, since you and Bunzee are here with us, is this not a special occasion?"

"Oh my goodness!" exclaimed Grandma. "I think you're right!" So together, they enjoyed fruits, vegetables, and the best chocolate cookie cakes she had ever tasted. They tasted a bit like her brownies!

Do you know what moderation means?

During the meal, a little blue Walkabeean called Zaiahzooloo reached out to give Bunzee a chocolate cookie cake.

"Oh, no!" Grandma gently scolded. "Creatures like Bunzee, called dogs, should never eat chocolate! It can make them very, very sick."

Little blue Zaiahbooloo sighed because he now knew this was not good. He was very sorry and promised never to do that again.

23

After dinner, the Walkabeeans wanted to show Grandma and Bunzee how they harvested cocoa beans and made them into cocoa powder. Once ground into powder, the beans had a very bitter flavor. The powder needed something sweet—like sugar—to make it taste so delicious.

A Walkabeean named Sweetszam and his twin sister, Snoogleegoo, told Grandma that God gave this very special cocoa treat to creatures like them because He loves them so much and wants them to enjoy treats once in a while. It also helps humans, like Grandma, with antioxidants and happiness for special events, like holidays and birthdays.

Grandma Bailee was grateful to hear about the benefits of chocolate. This must be why she liked to bake goodies for people—because it made them happy!

Do you know what an antioxidant is?

Grandma had noticed something about the creatures, and she wasn't sure what to do. All the Walkabeeans had very yellow teeth and unpleasant breath.

First, she said, "Come, I want to show you something very helpful." Then she made a game for the littlest Walkabeeans, Zaiahzooloo and Tootletoots, and their momma, Charcacao, to gather twine and sticks to make toothbrushes. Charcacao found some baking soda and fresh mint leaves that they used to bake goodies. Grandma then made a tube of homemade toothpaste. All the Walkabeeans gathered, and they brushed their teeth. Oh, what a sight to see their yellow teeth turn to a sparkling white!

To help the creatures remember to brush their teeth, Grandma made up a poem, and they learned it together:

God gave me teeth so that I can eat. It's okay to enjoy a few sweet treats, but I must remember to brush my teeth. I want my smile to always shine to touch a heart with joy sometime.

While the colorful, happy Walkabeeans shared their bright new smiles, Grandma Bailee and Bunzee slipped away into a cave where a stunning waterfall crashed down onto the rocks and glistened into a beautiful pool of water. Grandma and Bunzee knelt and prayed. "Dear God, we are so grateful for this amazing adventure and for our new furry friends. Please bless them, and we hope that someday we will see them again. Amen."

Grandma did not express the same words as before she was transported, "Sweetzsam, Snoogleegoo, Zaiahbooloo, Tootletoots." Instead, she said, "I am so blessed and can't wait to get back home where I will never again feel so alone, Kayleekat, Addiajoy, Petalpaiz, Zoe'booboo."

Without a thought, Grandma Bailee and Bunzee were transported back home through the pantry portal. Wow! Grandma wore a great big smile while looking down at Bunzee and holding a huge bag of cocoa powder. This bag would last a very long while.

She and Bunzee were so happy to be home, but Grandma felt a little sad that she did not get to say goodbye to her new friends, the Walkabeeans. Deep inside her heart, she knew she could go back again, and that made her heart feel warm and excited because we know Grandma Bailee loved adventures, and now, she loved the Walkabeeans.

Grandma Bailee felt peaceful and grinned; she could not wait to start baking yummy brownies for the new neighbors using the fresh cocoa powder the Walkabeeans helped her and Bunzee harvest and bring back to her sweet home on Cadbury Lane. After all, moving to a new home is a very special occasion, an adventure, and she wanted them to feel welcome and happy!

THE END

Questions & Answers

1. What is a cocoa pod?
    A pod is a hard-shell football-shaped fruit that safely holds about twenty to sixty seeds.

2. Is cocoa part of the fruit or vegetable family?
    The cocoa pod is known as the fruit of the tree.

3. What does moderation mean?
    To have self-discipline and self-control, to not use something excessively, which could be harmful otherwise.

4. What is an antioxidant?
   A helpful ingredient, such as vitamin C or E, that removes harmful matter within our bodies.

5. Bonus: Did you notice the flowers on some of the trees? The flowers do not last long on the cocoa trees and are pollinated not by bees but little flies called Forcipomyia midges. Without the midges, there would be no fruit.

Authors' Bio

Marissa Marie is a 2019 high school graduate who loves music, dance, travel, and is very adventurous. She is witty, smart, and her own person with wisdom beyond her years. Marissa is still contemplating her college major and currently works at Panera Bread.

LaNette is a speaker, trainer, writer, and vocalist. She has been married to her husband Ron for thirty-two years. LaNette has two daughters, one stepson, and eight blended grandchildren. She is the founder of ShyAnn's Hope, "restoring dignity, value, and healing to single moms," in memory of her heavenly daughter ShyAnn Marie.

From day one, LaNette fell deeply in love with her grandchildren. Without question, she knew spending quality memory-building time and praying for them was her God-given responsibility. LaNette prays that every grandma and grandpa will receive and respect this honor and gift of creating priceless love-filled memories with their grandchildren. Furthermore, she hopes that parents will respect this irreplaceable relationship and never withhold from their children this amazing character-building experience, even though there may be unresolved issues.

Illustrator's Bio

Michelle Adu-Asah is a Ghanaian and was born on June 18th 2001 in Bielefeld, Germany. She grew up with two wonderful parents and one big brother, who are all into art, designing, and creating things. Currently in Germany, she is training as a technical graphic design assistant in college and will complete her degree in 2020.

Her passion for illustrating digital art developed around 2016. Before then, she usually drew traditionally on paper. However, as her interest grew, she ventured into experimenting with programs like Adobe Photoshop, Illustrator, and Procreate; and now she draws cartoon portraits, cover artworks, T-shirt designs, and children's books. She had the honor of illustrating this book authored by LaNette Shipley and her granddaughter, Marissa, who live in the United States.

I hope you enjoy reading and have lots of fun.

—Michelle (@idraw_toon)

About the Book

Grandma Bailee loves adventure, but she never imagined what would happen to her while in the pantry one sunny summer Sunday afternoon.

With a koosh, kaash, swoosh, swaash, poof! Just like that, Grandma Bailee and her fur baby, Bunzee, disappeared through a pantry portal.

Where did they go? Who did they meet? And what did they learn? Find out in this first edition of Make Room for Grandma Bailee educational/adventure series Attack of the Walkabeeans.

Printed in the United States
By Bookmasters